VIKING BETRAYED

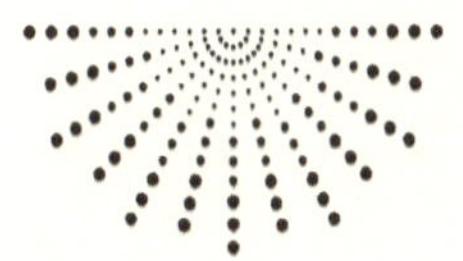

REE THORNTON

DEDICATION

For my sister Melissa who will always be my safe haven.

"I am smiling because we're sisters. I'm laughing because there is nothing you can do about it."
Anonymous

CHAPTER ONE

HILDA

he secrets and lies had to stop.

Warm spring sunshine beating down on her back, Hilda walked toward the well with the wooden pail in her hand, staring at the great hall that towered above the roofs of the ramshackle cottages that lined the streets of Visby. The imposing building served as both a declaration of Jarl Valen Eriksson's power and wealth, and a warning to any who would declare war on the isle of Gottland. But to her it was a daily reminder that she was deceiving those who had offered her a home, and though they did not know it, sanctuary.

This last month, the desire to tell Ulf the truth, to show him her scars and cast aside the ever-present shadow over her marriage, had become harder and harder to deny.

I must do it. Even though her nightmares had eased, the scars in her mind were just as deep and ugly as those her father had left on her body. Scars and pain that would never go away. She wanted Ulf to understand why she had hidden her body, to understand the reasons for the unspoken distance that hovered like a threatening storm cloud between them. Swallowing the hard lump that had formed in her throat, Hilda firmed her resolve. It was time to be honest about her past. *I shall tell him after the evening meal.* Ulf was a good husband, he deserved to know the truth.

"Murderer!"

Startled, Hilda slipped into an alcove in the rough stone wall that surrounded the bustling town of Visby and peered out. She had been so deeply in thought that she had not noticed the angry hum of the crowd gathered on the grass in front of Jarl Eriksson's longhouse. She loathed the trapped sensation that accompanied the press of bodies in a large crowd, but she was curious about the commotion interrupting the usual routine of daily chores.

"Dirty thief!"

Thief. The pail slipped from her fingers, her pulse quickening until it sounded like a dozen horses galloping in a deafening rhythm as the shouted insult rang out over the muffled jeering of the crowd.

Raising up on her tiptoes, Hilda searched for Ulf. *By the gods, don't let him be hurt.* As head stonemason, Ulf oversaw the construction of the wall that protected the town. Deep in her gut she knew that her husband would be at the center of this commotion, since he took such pride in defending the wall and the town within too.

Squeezing her eyes tight, she sagged against the wall when she spotted his broad shoulders barrelling through the crowd.

Ulf was so tall that he towered above the rowdy mob, his handsome features darkened by his somber expression and his golden hair pulled back into a messy knot with a leather tie. Indeed, Ulf was large all over. Blessed Freya, everything about Ulf was hot, and hard, and impressive.

A stone skittered across the ground nearby.

Hilda snapped back to reality. *Who was that?*

A little girl bounced along in her small boots and a dirty play dress, her messy hair escaping her braid and flying out behind her as she chatted to the handsewn toy in her hand.

Hilda looked around. *Where is her mother?* She should not be out here alone with the rowdy crowd so close by. And the garden was too dangerous a place for one so young.

The child skipped across the grass toward the overgrown and neglected garden that had become a favorite hiding place for children avoiding their chores.

After they had wed, Ulf had told her very firmly that the garden was his brother Ivvár's territory and to stay out of it when she had suggested it needed clearing and replanting. Given Ivvár spent all of his time raiding and chasing women it was unlikely the garden would be tamed anytime soon. Nevertheless, she had relented since the last thing she needed was to cause strife and draw attention to herself.

"Put a sword through him!"

Hilda's eyes darted back to the angry mob where the mood had deteriorated even further. When wronged, Viking men were quick to temper and favored settling matters with blades. A dark sense of foreboding crept up her spine at the sight of her husband making his way through the melee.

The crowd parted in front of him, nobody willing to confront the brawny Viking who resembled a son of the giantess Skaði, descendent of the Frost Giants. Only a fool would cause trouble with an Eriksson and risk the wrath of all of the brothers.

"Blood for blood," a brave soul dared cry out.

"Silence." Ulf's shout cut through the murmurs of agreement, then he tugged hard on the length of rope he held in one hand.

A man came into view, hands bound and stumbling wildly. Finding his balance, the man yanked on the rope defiantly and glared up at his towering captor.

Hilda froze, air rushing from her lungs, her eyes riveted on the prisoner as clawing suffocation tore at her chest.

Father?

"Nei," she whimpered, and shrank back into the shadows. He *couldn't* be here. She peered out again and her eyes confirmed what her head already knew. It *was* him. She pressed fully back into the alcove, a sob escaping her dry lips. She could not let him see her, not when she had risked her life to make him believe she was dead. To escape her father's beatings, she'd pretended to lose her footing on a bridge and thrown herself into a flooded river. She'd welcomed the bitter cold as she'd sunk below the surface and surrendered to the rushing current hurtling her downstream. At the time she'd been convinced that death was better than enduring another day beneath his roof.

Unable to help herself, Hilda peered around the jagged edge of the wall, as jagged as the nerves in her belly.

"Leave off," Ulf roared, and waved his hand at the crowd. "There will be no killing this day. Ubbi Tannrsson will face the laws as is his right."

The crowd roared in protest. They wanted blood, and right-fully so.

Hand on her stomach, Hilda struggled to breathe through her nausea. Why had she thought she could tell Ulf? Who would forgive a thief, a woman who had spied on and then betrayed the people of Visby? His people. And now hers. He would never forgive her for what she had done—not that she deserved his forgiveness. But she was trying to leave that all in her past. She had changed. Yet there was still the lie, so many lies. Lies that stole any spark of happiness she began to feel in this new life she was building with Ulf. Lies that she could not escape.

Even hidden safely behind the stone alcove, her hands trembled, and she could not tear her gaze from the man she despised. Hilda picked at her thumbnail, starting with the edge right near the skin. She was aware she was doing it, but she couldn't stop herself. Even the pain of the skin tearing didn't stop her fingers worrying at it. If her father discovered she was still alive, her life was over. He would never accept her marriage to Ulf. She had no doubt that he would lash out in spite and reveal all of the secrets she had fought so hard to conceal, then he would force her to return to Kalmar, or worse, steal for him again.

Crossing his arms over his broad chest, Ulf stood glaring until the crowd began to disperse. He was a fearsome warrior, her husband, and unless she did something, the love she saw in his eyes would soon turn to wrath.

Hilda bit her lip and wiped her sweaty hands on her dress. She could not let him discover her secret. She would lose everything. She would lose him.

As the last few stoic objectors moved away, Ulf tugged her father forward and bent to tighten the rope restraining him.

Hilda looked up at the towering wall that circled the city of Visby, a desperate plan forming in her mind. She wanted her father gone, as far from here as possible. She needed to cause a distraction so he could escape. If she were careful, neither he nor Ulf would ever know she was responsible. It would work. Her father would pounce on the first opportunity to flee, she was sure of it.

Yanking her hood up to hide her face, she crept silently along the wall toward the stone steps that led up to the north guard tower. It was empty now—the guard having left his post a short while ago to make his rounds along the wall. Once inside she would grab one of the bows and run along the top of the wall, shooting arrows just close enough to cause a distraction before disappearing into the crowded market yonder. She glanced around furtively, reassuring herself that nobody had noticed her cloaked figure as she bounded deftly up the uneven stone steps.

Splash!

"Nei," a child whined miserably.

Hilda froze mid-step and glanced toward the noise.

On the far side of the grassy lawn, the young girl now stood beside the well, the top half of her body on the ledge as she strained to look inside.

Hilda's heart jumped to her throat.

Her desperate glance went to Ulf and her father. Then swung back to the child. Her hand curled into a fist and then she punched it into her thigh, hard. A groan escaped her lips at the impossible decision she now faced—help her father escape and protect her secret or save the child. She couldn't do both. Loki and his cursed tricks! She had to choose, fast.

The little girl grunted as she got her foot up onto the ledge and levered herself up. She stood up on unsteady feet atop the rocky ledge.

Hel! If the child fell in the well, she would die! Time slowed and she held her breath.

The girl leaned forward to look down into the darkness for her missing toy, and her foot slipped on the rock.

In a heartbeat, Hilda jumped from the steps and sprinted forward as the child's arms waved in a frantic struggle to regain her balance. She wasn't going to make it to the child in time. She pumped her arms faster, her feet thundering across the grass. She'd have to jump. If anyone saw her there would be questions, but she had no choice. She'd been jumping across rooftops wider than this since she was a child. She could do it.

The girl toppled forward.

Pushing off with all her might, Hilda leapt, her arms outstretched, and slammed into the stone ledge. The air rushed from her lungs at the impact that felt like it had broken ribs, then her fingers snagged on fabric and she clenched her hand into a fist.

The girl let out a high-pitched squeal of terror as she swung in the air and slammed into the side of the well.

"Hold on. I have you. I have you." Reaching out, Hilda grabbed the girl's tiny arm and hauled her up, slumping on the ground beside the well with the trembling pale child in her arms.

"Jóra! Oh! Jóra!" Dina, the carpenter's wife, ran toward them, her eyes wide with terror. The woman fell to her knees and pulled the sobbing child from Hilda's arms.

"Are you hurt?" Dina asked her daughter, her hands searching limbs for injuries.

"Nei, Mumma."

"Thank the gods." She wrapped the child in a tight embrace. "Thank you, Hilda. Thank you for saving her."

Hilda nodded at the grateful mother, her heart warming at the gratitude in the woman's eyes. As more people who were alerted by the child's cries arrived, Hilda rose to her feet, absently responding to those who clutched her arm and patted her shoulder. Rising up on her toes, she craned her neck to see over the gathering crowd, her heart sinking as she watched her father disappear through the doorway that led to the prisoners' cells. She was too late.

Her one chance...gone.

CHAPTER TWO

ULF

The dark shadows of night had long settled over the quiet village of Visby when Ulf was wrenched from sleep. *Was that a foot kicking him?*

"Nei. Father," Hilda moaned as she tossed back and forth beside him, her legs twisting in the thick woollen blanket they shared.

Father? He looked across at her, his mood darkening at the sight of her pained expression. On their wedding night, he had discovered that someone had harmed her when she had refused to unrobe when they made love for the first time. Determined to prove he would not hurt her, he had used his lips and hands until she was breathless, and then taken her with gentle tenderness. Afterward, he had held her in his arms, satisfied that she would soon come to trust him, but then the nightmares began. That night, and every night thereafter for many moons, she was plagued by a darkness in her spirit. Nowadays, she responded to his touch with an equal ardor, and their lovemaking would be perfect but for the fact that she still refused to undress. At first, he had pushed her for answers and been hurt when she stubbornly refused to discuss it at all. He was her husband, they were supposed to share their troubles and overcome them together. That's what marriage was, what he wanted from their relationship. Eventually the nightmares had eased, and he had stopped asking about them, content that whatever ailed her had faded.

But now they were back.

He raised himself up on an elbow and looked down at her. By the gods she was beautiful. Her long dark hair was a mass of tangled auburn curls that fell across the pale green shift that covered her curves. Even with her sharp features and full lips contorted by whatever haunted her dreams, his manhood surged to life at the sight of her. He still could not believe he was wed to a woman as kind and beautiful as his high-born wife. Until he had married Hilda, he had always felt overshadowed by his brothers, less worthy. He did not possess the power or riches of his eldest brother Valen, who was Jarl. He had not the thirst for blood or riches that drove men to war and raiding, and would never achieve the glory and fame of a warrior like his other brothers. He was content with his life as a stonemason, a craftsman. Yet Hilda had chosen him. He brushed the damp hair from her forehead.

"Hilda," he whispered, and when she did not respond, he shook her gently to free her from whatever haunted her dreams.

"Nei." Throwing her hands up in front of her face, she pushed back against an imaginary attack. "Nei."

"Hilda." He shook her harder. "Wake up."

She snapped upright, her hand darting out to the night table. A heartbeat later she had her dagger against his throat, the tip digging into his soft flesh.

"Hilda," he croaked out, not wanting to scare her into further action.

"Ulf?" She inhaled a sharp pained gasp and dropped the dagger on the bedding, her whole body shaking as she looked around, her green eyes wide with fear and confusion.

Picking up the blade, he placed it on his night table beside his own. His heart ached that after a full year of marriage she still did not feel safe with him, but she had never pulled a blade on him, never. He hid his concern. "Are you alright?" he asked, caressing her arm gently.

She brushed his hand away. "It is just a dream."

Ulf sighed heavily. She always pushed him away after an episode. If only she would talk to him, he would gladly share her burden. "It has been a long while since the last bad one. Do you want to talk?"

"Not now, husband." She stared straight ahead, her forefinger and thumb plucking at a stray thread on the woollen blanket.

"But—" Why had the dreams returned? Was this a one off, or would they come back with the same frequency as before? He couldn't bear to think of her tormented even in her dreams, and it troubled him that she would not share her burden. He'd been patient, but he hated secrets, hated them. He was her husband, he wanted to share everything, yet she insisted on keeping this distance between them. He didn't understand it, nor her reasons for doing so.

"Leave it, Ulf."

"It is not my nature and you know it. I hate that something is wrong and I cannot fix it."

"Naught is wrong."

"Gods, Hilda. Don't lie to me. Why can you not trust me with this?"

"I do trust you." Her tone had lost the defensiveness of earlier, now softer, and laden with sadness.

"Nei. If you did you would talk to me. What could have happened to the daughter of a nobleman that is so bad it keeps her up at night?"

An uncomfortable silence surrounded them, pushing out and filling the room until it felt suffocating.

"I would that it were so easy," she said in a soft whisper, her voice strained.

"Have I not proven you can trust me? I've been a good husband, já?" he asked, though in his heart he knew the answer. She would not be crying out for her dead father if she were satisfied being his wife.

He glanced down at his hands covered in the scars and callouses of long hours carving stone. He was lucky she even let him touch her.

"Do not ask this of me, I beg you," she said, her voice catching before she turned away.

Ulf looked across at her slender back, the dip of her waist and curve of her hips. And that bottom. Gods, he loved the firm globes of her ass. He ached to hold her breasts in his hands as he rocked in and out of her, but that blasted shift was always in the way. He'd known she was haunted when they'd married, damaged by a past she never spoke of, but he'd never imagined she would still refuse to bare herself to him after a year as husband and wife. He couldn't chase away the nightmares, but as her husband he would offer her the comfort of his arms. No wife of his would leave his bed unsatisfied.

"Come here." He rolled over and pulled her into his arms, until her bottom nestled firmly against his hard length. "I want to love you."

She hummed in approval when he kissed the crook of her neck and sucked on her earlobe.

He slid his hand over one of her heavy breasts, cupping it and squeezing before he teased the nipple through the fabric. She loved it when he did that.

"Touch me, Ulf," she begged. She rocked back against his

hardness, and then her hand reached back to grip him, sliding back and forth in the seductive rhythm she knew he loved.

He slid her hem up and caressed her legs and thighs, careful never to wander above the waist. He wanted to taste her on his tongue but had not the patience to wait. His fingers dipped between her thighs and into the wet heat that signalled her readiness for him.

"Já." It was a breathless needy moan. "More."

Fingers stroking her tender flesh, he teased until she was panting with need, until she was slick and writhed against him desperately. Then he gripped his swollen rod and guided himself into her.

"Gods, Hilda. That feels so good." He cupped her bottom in his hands and looked down at where they joined, mesmerized by the sight of his cock sinking into her tight heat.

"Oh. Já," she whispered when he slid out slowly then thrust in hard, his hips slamming against her behind.

He reached around to tease her swollen nub, taking her time and time again to the brink of release but never allowing her to crest.

Soon she was begging. "Please, more, more."

"Roll over, wife," he growled. He wanted to look into her eyes when he filled her with his seed. He wanted to watch as she was swept away on the wave of pleasure so he could enjoy the rapture on her features. The rapture he gave her. He pulled her leg up over his waist and sank back inside her. His fingers toyed with the strap of her nightshift, edging it slowly down her shoulder in the hope that this would be the night that she would let him remove it.

"Nei." She shrugged his hand off, denying him as she pressed her mouth to his, her tongue flicking against his in a tantalizing dance.

He held her head in his hands, his fingers tangling in her hair as he plundered her mouth, allowing her no quarter. Never had a woman ignited such a fire in his loins as his Hilda. It had always been like this between them in the bedchamber, him unleashing his need to conquer her body, and her willingly surrendering to his domination. He always reached for her first, controlled the pace and her pleasure. He loved it when she moaned as he held her hands above her head—he'd lose all reason and pound into her until she clamped around him and he saw stars.

Hilda broke the kiss. "Take me," she whispered.

Wrapping his hand around her hair like he knew she loved, he growled in her ear and withdrew. "Are you telling me what to do, wife?" He slammed back in, his hips surging forward in a relentless rhythm.

Her hands curled around his arms, her hips rising and falling to match his pace.

Gods, she felt good. That intense pleasure with just a taste of darkness and danger.

She was close now, her nails digging into his arm, her breathing panting and desperate.

"Open your eyes," he demanded, stilling inside her. He would not let her hide her eyes from him when he was inside her—on this he would not waver. It mattered not that she hid her body from him. If he could see her eyes, she couldn't hide from him. And their connection in that perfect moment was enough. For now.

"Nei. Don't stop." Slowly her dark lashes fluttered open and she looked up at him, her eyes shimmering like the emerald gem-encrusted dagger he'd bought for her from a Rus trader.

"Gods, Hilda. You slay me." One hand slid down to pluck at her pebbled nipples through her shift as he resumed the rhythm that had her melting beneath him. They moved as one, their eyes locked, her body arching for his touch as he loved her until he was breathless, his skin glistening with sweat.

A long throaty moan fell from her lips as she froze, her

whole body shuddering as she pulsed around him. Throwing one hand up over her head, she dug her fingers into the pillow and thrust her breasts up, looking every bit a flame-haired goddess as her eyes closed and she surrendered to her release.

"Já." His heart expanded at the sight of her shattering, the unreserved joy on her face loosening all his restraint. With his arms either side of her shoulders he hovered above her, his gaze fixed on the vision below him as he spilled his seed within her. Then, as the waves of ecstasy ebbed, he collapsed on the bed and gathered her close, frustrated with the fabric that kept him from feeling her skin against his, that kept him from feeling all of her.

Sighing contentedly, Hilda settled in his arms.

"Sleep, wife," he said, and held her close until she slumbered peacefully.

Ulf lay awake until the sun rose on the horizon. Making love usually kept the unease at bay, but for the first time it had not worked. It gnawed at him from the inside, an annoying relentless niggle that would not abate. He felt sick to his stomach, just like when Elin, the second daughter of Jarl Torbjorn Sjurnssen, had feigned affection and then used him to get close to Valen. Her deceit had caused chaos, pitting brother against brother until it was discovered and his father had sent her away. He was still licking his wounds when Hilda came into his life, and then just as he had fallen in love with her, she was gone. When she had returned three moons later, he'd been so glad to see her again and so sure that she loved him, that he'd been willing to overlook everything else. She was a noble woman, he had reasoned. Graceful and reserved was the person she was. And then after he had realized she had been hurt, he'd not wanted to push her boundaries. He had been patient for a full year, and then had hoped when the dreams ceased that she would one day share what haunted her with him. But now the nightmares were back.

He rolled over and saw the dagger he had taken from her.

She had held a dagger to his throat in their bed! This was not a healthy marriage, her not trusting him and him allowing it—it clearly wasn't working. Giving her at least a few hours of sleep without the nightmares was no longer enough. He wanted their marriage to be more. He wanted all of her.

CHAPTER THREE

HILDA

The scent of warm bread and honey tickled her nostrils. Stretching her arms up over her head, Hilda chased the sleep from her bones. She loved lying in on these cool mornings with the sweet scent of the fresh spring air wafting through the window. It was time to plant the garden, so that they would have fresh greens over the summer months and root vegetables to store for next winter.

"Good. You're awake." The bed dipped as Ulf sat down and placed a steaming cup of pine needle tea and a plate on the small table beside her.

"What is this?" Pushing herself upright, Hilda looked at his thoughtful offering then back at him. "It is not like you to bring me tea and breakfast in bed. Normally I am the one feeding you."

"I know. Drink it while it is still hot," he said, picking up the warm tea and handing it to her.

Smiling at him fondly, she sipped, enjoying the balance of freshness with the honey he had added. He knew just how she liked it. Ulf was a good husband, but rarely pampered her like this and she suspected he wanted something in return for his efforts. She quirked an eyebrow at him and waited for him to answer her unasked question.

He lightly fingered a loose tendril of her hair before tucking it behind her ear. "I wanted to talk to you about last night."

The heat she'd felt at his touch disappeared in an instant and she looked down into her tea, afraid that her eyes would betray her guilt. "It was just a dream."

"Stop, Hilda." He picked up her free hand, cradling it gently in his and caressing her palm with his thumb. "Have I not been patient? Come now, it is time to have no secrets. Nothing in your past can hurt you here. We cannot continue like this."

"Like what?" *Don't say it. Don't say it.* But she knew he would. She could see it in his tense shoulders and the firm set of his jaw. Last night, she'd pulled a blade on him, and Ulf would want answers.

"It is time to talk about your past, and the reason for these nightmares. We cannot continue with you keeping secrets from me. It's like there is a whole other part of you that you keep from me."

She swallowed hard. The words would not come. Because they would destroy her marriage. "A woman must have her secrets," she said, attempting a coy smile.

"Gods, Hilda. Don't jest." He pinned her with such a disappointed stare that her guilt swelled and crashed down over her. "You refuse to tell me why you have bad dreams. We have been married a year and I have yet to see your body. I am a man, Hilda." He pounded a fist against his chest. "I want to see my wife naked, touch her body, know what is in her mind. Your secrets are hurting us."

"Why are you like this?" she demanded. "Why can my dreams not stay secret?"

He stiffened, then looked at her thoughtfully before he

spoke. "The last woman that hid things from me almost destroyed my family."

"What did she do?"

"She let me court her, let me think that we would be married, when what she really wanted was to get close to Valen. She wanted to wed a Jarl."

Hilda froze, shocked. He'd never mentioned another woman, not once. She'd always assumed there had been others before her, but not any that meant anything to him. This was bad, even worse than she'd thought. There was no way she could tell him now. How could he understand?

"Why do you not trust me?"

Stomach clenching and heart racing, Hilda picked her thumb and scrambled desperately for an explanation Ulf would believe. "I do trust you—"

"Nei. You don't." He shook his head, his gaze clouded with wounded hurt that made her heart race.

What was she to do? She licked her parched lips, attempting to quell her rising panic. She didn't want to lie to him anymore. She loathed hurting the only person who had ever cared for her, loved her. Would he still want her after he learned that she was a liar, a fraud? A cold shiver spread over her as her father's face flashed in her mind, his dark eyes glowing as he hurt her, the cruel twist of his mouth. *Nei.* She could not do it. Trusting men led to pain, lots of it. The hard lump in her stomach reminded her that she had always known that it would come to this, that one day he would ask her for what she could not give. Her heart thundered in her ears as she sought a way to escape this conversation without destroying their life together. But there was nothing.

"I want to trust you." After she said it, she realized it was true. She wanted to trust him. She didn't know if she could, but she wanted to, which was more than she'd ever wanted with anyone else.

He crossed his arms over his chest and leaned back. "Then prove it."

Reaching for his hand, Hilda entwined their fingers and gently brushed her thumb over his calloused palm. "I do want to trust you, I promise. But…it is painful to talk of these things. Please don't ask that of me."

"Gods, Hilda." He pulled his hand from hers, leaving her feeling bereft. "It is not too much to ask for my wife to share what troubles her, to share her body. Hel, to share *anything*. I cannot abide secrets, not again. I need you to be honest with me."

Hilda sagged back against the pillow, leaning her head back on the bedhead. This was it. His expression was so aggrieved, so earnest, that she knew Ulf was not going to let it go this time. She could not fault him, for any other man would have insisted on answers long ago. She released a heavy sigh. Ulf deserved an explanation, but the truth would tear them apart and she could not bear to lose him. Could she give him some of her story, just enough to show she trusted him without giving away too much?

Biting her lip, Hilda nodded. "You are right. I owe you answers."

His eyes widened at her acquiescence, the silence stretching between them.

Such was the tender affection in his eyes that she resolved to trust him. She would show him her scars, the ugly evidence of her father's wrath, without revealing the truth of how she got them. Until she knew Ulf would not forsake her, she would not reveal the truth that would expose her lies.

"When?" he asked.

The light in his eyes dimmed when she shook her head. "You must get to work. I shall tell you this eve."

"In truth, this eve?"

"Já. I swear it." Fighting back her rising panic, she smiled at him reassuringly. Blessed Freya give her the strength to keep her vow.

Ulf nodded in satisfaction and rose to his feet. "Until this eve then," he said, and then kissed her on the forehead and strode from the room.

Hilda let her head fall into her hands. *Could she do it?*

CHAPTER FOUR

ULF

Ulf rounded the corner and strode toward his cottage, smiling at the warm glow shining through the window and the brief shadow of Hilda moving about inside. As he'd washed away the dirt and dust of a long day's work in the bathhouse all he could think about was Hilda and her promise to be honest with him.

"Wife," he said, smiling gently at Hilda as he kicked off his boots and placed them inside the door.

"Ulf," she said, then continued preparing the evening meal, her actions awkward and stiff and gaze wary.

His eyes moved down over the forest green dress that clung to the creamy swell of her breasts, his fingers itching to peel it from her luscious curves.

"The food is ready. Sit," she said, placing a mug of ale in his hands.

Throwing one last admiring glace her way, he walked to the small table by the window and lowered himself into the seat, one arm slung over the armrest.

Hilda moved around the kitchen, the light from the over-head lanterns flickering across her pale face as she served the meal onto two trenchers. Her shaking hands betrayed her nervousness, and then his eyes caught on her bloody thumb, scratched raw from her picking. She bit her bottom lip and persevered, so he said nothing.

Downing the ale, he placed the cup on the table. He had to believe that she would feel better once she had shared what ailed her, and that would come soon enough. For now, he just wanted to share a simple meal with his wife. He watched the gentle sway of her hips as she walked toward him, his blood heating as her plump breasts almost spilled out of her dress as she bent to set the meal before him. Without even trying she lit a fire in his veins like no other woman ever had.

"Roasted duck?" he said, his mouth watering at the succulent aromas wafting from the table.

"Já. I know it is your favorite. Eat," she said, waving at him to begin as she sat across from him and filled their mugs.

They chatted, as they always did, about the events of the day in between bites, though the knowledge of what was to come weighed heavy in the air between them.

After eating, Ulf reclined on the rug by the fireplace, his legs crossed at the ankles, and waited. He could hear her moving around behind him, shuffling back and forth under the guise of tidying as she delayed. Looking into the flames, he resisted the urge to call her over, to make it easier for her.

A short while later, he heard her suck in a shaky breath, and then she walked to stand in front of him, the flames of the fire behind her making her auburn hair glow.

"You were right. We cannot continue this way."

He said nothing, holding her gaze as he waited for her to continue.

"I…" Her voice wavered as she finally found the words. "It is hard for me to talk of this. Any man I have trusted has hurt me."

"You can trust me, Hilda. I will not hurt you. Have I not

proven that? There is naught you say that will change how I feel about you. I promise. I love you."

He watched her inhale a shuddering breath and her eyes drifted closed. He could almost hear her mind ticking over.

"Keeping it inside is hurting you, love."

~

*U*lf was right, keeping this pain inside hurt. Even ignored, it felt like a huge hole in her chest, and then remembering was like the cut of a thousand blades at once. She could not escape it, even in her sleep. She would never be able to move on until she faced it.

"You can tell me. Whatever it is, you can tell me."

He was a good man. Too good for her. It was just a matter of time before he was lured from her bed by another woman, a woman who could satisfy him and give him what she could not. All day she had battled with herself about telling him the truth, but she couldn't do it. It would crush him. The less Ulf knew the better. She needed to stick to her plan. It was a good plan, one that she hoped would get her through this with her marriage intact.

You will lose him. The warning was a harsh whisper in her head. She knew it was true. Even if he was not repelled by her ugly scars, he would hate her when he discovered the depth of her lies. It was better this way. Give him enough half-truths to satisfy him and keep him from asking more questions. She could not bear to lose the only person who loved her. As selfish as it was, she could not let him go, not yet.

Hilda opened her eyes and met his blue ones, then nodded. Ulf loved her. Not a day had passed where he had not shown her that in small thoughtful ways. She owed him this.

Heat flared in Ulf's eyes, then hope, as he recognized her decision. He would get his answers, finally.

"There was a man…" It came out in a rushed breath that surprised her. "He cornered me one night and hurt me. He did not want to use my body for pleasure, he…" The tears pooling in her eyes burned as she struggled to hold them back. "He enjoyed causing pain, and he hurt me."

Ulf's jaw clenched and he sat upright, but he held her gaze, and the understanding she saw there gave her the courage to continue.

"He beat me, badly. There was nothing I could do to stop him," she choked out.

"Is this what you dream of? Him?"

She nodded.

"Who is he?" he demanded. "I will kill him."

"He is dead. My father found me and killed him for what he had done." The lie left a foul taste in her mouth.

The tension eased from his shoulders and he looked up at her, his expression resolute. "I am sorry this happened to you. Not all men are like that, Hilda. I would never hurt a woman. I would never hurt you."

"I know that now. There is more. I keep my shift on because I have…" She stumbled for a moment before pushing aside her final doubts and pressing on. "Because I have scars, many scars." The thought of what was to come, of baring herself to him was terrifying.

"Hilda…" Ulf sat up. His voice was gruff and raspy, laced with pain as it trailed off.

"I would hide nothing from you now." Slowly, she undid the ornate silver brooches that fastened her tunic, her fingers trembling as she forced herself to stay the course.

Ulf leaned back and gazed into her eyes as her dress fell to her feet and she stepped out of it.

Inside she was falling to pieces, but she could not look away. Her stomach dropped when Ulf remained motionless, his face an unreadable mask. Freya help her, was this a mistake?

"You would have all of me..." She lifted her underdress over her head and tossed it aside, her nipples instantly furling into tight buds beneath her soft shift.

"All of you?" Swallowing hard, his eyes roamed over her figure, and when they returned to hers, they were lit with such hunger that her heart skipped.

Hilda nodded. "Even the parts I cannot leave behind or ever forget." Hands shaking, she lifted the thin fabric that she had hidden behind for so long, up and over her head. The soft whoosh of it falling at her feet was as deafening as the hammering of her heart. Lifting her chin, she fought back the urge to hide her gaze from him.

"Even my scars."

He inhaled sharply at the sight of the silvery marks that crisscrossed her alabaster skin. Though her full breasts hung heavy, the tight nipples begging for his attention, his eyes were drawn to the mass of old wounds that covered her stomach. She knew that it was a horrible sight. Even the tender sides of her hips had not been spared and puckered scars where she had been whipped covered her back too.

A string of curses fell from his mouth as his hands tightened into fists.

"I know it is ugly," she said, her hands moving to cover herself and her gaze dropping to her feet.

"Now I understand why you would not unrobe." He rose to his feet and crossed to her in two strides. The warm palm of his hand cupped her chin and tilted her head back until her eyes met his.

"There is no shame in the scars that made you who you are, Hilda," he whispered softly.

A hot tear ran down her cheek and she sniffled.

"All will be well. He cannot hurt you anymore."

Her breath caught as his fingers traced over the long silvery scar that ran along the underside of her right breast.

"You are more beautiful than I imagined."

Gods, how she had longed to hear him say that. She had dreaded that he would see only the scars and not the woman beneath. She was wrong to fear that he would find her ugly, disfigured, broken. Nestling in against his chest, she wound her hands around his waist and kissed the hollow of his neck.

"Ulf, please," she murmured, pressing against the evidence of his desire. Her heart thumped erratically. She wanted to feel his hands on her body, feel him inside her and know that he wanted her despite her imperfections.

Lifting her by her bottom, Ulf stumbled backward and sat on the table. "When the moonlight kisses your flesh your scars shimmer and dance like the green lights that dance across the sky in the harvest season. Beautiful."

"Kiss me," Hilda whispered, the longing in her voice matching the heat in her eyes.

"Gods, Hilda," he groaned, his eyes falling closed as he pressed his mouth to her in a searing kiss.

Ulf's arms tightened around her, and she opened to him, surrendering to his demanding lips until her senses reeled. She inhaled sharply as his fingers gently explored her scarred back. Images flashed in her mind—fists, blood, and the crack of bones breaking. Her back bowed, sharp pain coursing through her body.

"Nei," she whimpered, sliding off his lap and scampering away.

"Hilda?"

Holding her hands across her bared breasts, Hilda swept her discarded shift from the floor.

"Nei." He pulled the shift from her trembling hands, then swept her into his arms and carried her into their bedchamber. Pulling back the covers roughly, he placed her on the bed.

The breath she didn't even realize she had been holding escaped when he pulled the covers over her nakedness. The soft fabric against her skin was like a soothing balm to her frayed nerves. Her heart sank as she finally realized the truth—the hidden scars were much worse than those on her skin.

A few moments later, he slid in behind her, his warm hand sliding across her stomach and pulling her back against him. "I love all of who you are, Hilda." His fingertips traced over the scars on her back.

The tension eased from her body at his soothing touch.

His fingers did not stray from her scars, the soft repetitive motions assuring her that he was offering comfort, not pleasure.

Hilda relaxed into the reassurance of his warm embrace, relieved that it was over, that she had bared her scars and satisfied his curiosity.

Ulf pressed a tender kiss on her shoulder blade, then another, and another, working his way upward until his lips pressed into the crook of her neck.

Smiling, she sighed contentedly.

Each touch felt like a whisper of devotion that he wielded like his sword to cut through the distance that had long separated them.

"I am glad that you trust me. I will not let you down."

The words, uttered low and husky in a promise, crashed down over her like ice cold water. No amount of his warmth could penetrate the cold core growing within her, because she was a liar, still.

A liar and a terrible wife.

CHAPTER FIVE

ULF

Though the morning was crisp and sunny, Ulf couldn't erase last night's events from his mind. Hilda walked at his side, her hand in his as they made their way across the settlement to the great hall.

"What is wrong, Ulf?" Usually they enjoyed their morning walk, using it as a chance to catch up, reflect, and plan. Today was different. They both could feel it.

"I am glad that you were honest with me and showed me your scars." He should be content that Hilda had finally shared her body, that she had been honest with him and tried to make love unclothed, but he wasn't.

"But?"

"But I am disappointed that we could not make love. That you do not trust me enough for that."

Hilda looked at him thoughtfully. "It reminds you of how you feel when you are with your brothers," she guessed.

He nodded and looked away. Try as he might, he could not shake the melancholy that had taken hold of him. He loved his brothers, but they were all warriors renowned for their skill in battle and raiding, and he was not. Though he trained with them daily and was a skilled swordsman, he had no desire to seek out conflict. He would defend Visby with vengeance, but otherwise preferred to build and create rather than cut down and destroy. His kin had never faulted him for it, yet he couldn't help but compare himself to his brothers and feel lacking. Marrying Hilda, knowing that a noble woman wanted him for a husband, had been validating and soothed some of his past hurts away. But even in that he had failed.

"Do you remember the day we met?"

Hilda smiled and nodded at two warriors, Múli and Einarr, as they passed by, then turned to him. "In the market?"

He nodded, squeezing her hand gently. "I remember it like it was yesterday. You wore that blue dress, your hair loose around your shoulders. All I could see of you was your back and your hands flailing around as you argued with Mikkel over an apple."

A soft smile tugged at the corners of her mouth. "He was trying to swindle me, and I was not having it."

"Mikkel has a knack for deception and overcharging."

"I thought you looked like Óðinn marching over to rescue me. I've never seen a man backpedal as swiftly as Mikkel did that day."

"When you looked up at me and smiled, I knew you were meant to be mine, and me yours. I thought then everything would be so great, but it is not. You did not trust me last night. You did not do as you promised."

"I tried."

He stopped and looked down into her eyes. "I know you did. We have time, but I need to know that it is not always going to be this way, that one day we will be able to make love as husband and wife with nothing between us."

"I want that too."

Tucking a stray hair behind her ear, he brushed his lips across hers. "We will go slow, my love. As slow as you need."

"I will try harder," she said softly.

"We both will," he assured her. "I am glad we are working on this. Another thirty years of this would destroy us and harm our family."

She jerked back as the truth of his words hit her. She knew as well as he that it was unlikely their marriage would ever survive in this state until they were old, and that any child raised in a troubled home did not thrive. She wanted a baby—they both did.

"I would not do that to our children, Hilda."

"Nor would I. We will try again."

Squeezing her hand, he smiled at her warmly. "We can do this together. I am sure of it. Now let's go break fast. I am starved."

CHAPTER SIX

HILDA

*H*ilda sat beside Ulf in the great hall and pushed the food around her plate. Her usually healthy appetite had disappeared.

At this hour, the hall was a hive of activity. Mothers feeding hungry children before ushering them outside to play and the men discussing the day's work as they broke their fast.

Normally Hilda would find comfort in the mundane scene that had been absent from her own childhood, but this morn she felt sick to her stomach.

"Wife, you must eat if you plan to join the hunting party today," Ulf said kindly, his mood much improved by their earlier conversation.

"I shall." Picking up some bread and cheese, she looked at the dais where Ulf's brother, Valen, sat finishing his meal.

The Jarl's focus was on his wife, Samara, and the young boy sitting on her lap devouring a juicy orange. Wrinkles crinkled the corners of his eyes as he laughed and wiped the sticky juice from the boy's hands and looked at his wife with obvious adoration. The Jarl's love match with his royal bride from the exotic lands of the east had inspired many songs by the travelling bards who visited Gottland.

Hilda wished she could know them better. Samara had tried to befriend her, but like everyone, Hilda kept her at a distance, afraid she would probe into her past and catch her out in a lie. Relaxing back into her chair, she reached for an apple. All was not lost. Her father was locked up in a cell and must have no idea that she was here, otherwise Valen would be calling on her for answers.

"I will go on the hunting trip," she said, turning to Ulf. It would be best to avoid town until her father went before Valen for judgement and justice was served. Her father would die, she had no doubt. Death was the only punishment for outlaws who continued to prey on settlements. She had no wish to see him die, but nor would she mourn him if that was his fate. At least if she went on the hunting trip and stayed away until it was done, her secret would die with her father and she would finally be safe.

"How long will you be gone?"

"Two days." She bit into the delicious crispy apple, her appetite returning now that she had a plan.

As the last of the tables were being cleared, the door slammed open, letting in a blast of air heavy with the promise of a spring storm.

A chill raced up her spine as a warrior dragged a bedraggled and beaten man into the great hall.

Ulf rose to his feet beside her. "What is the meaning of this, Kal? I told you to leave him alone. He should be in his cell until Valen calls for him." He shook his head at Visby's finest sword-smith, a man liked and respected by all.

Kal glowered. "I would have justice for my son. I shall not rest while this murderer still breathes," he said, pulling the prisoner's head back and holding a blade to his throat.

The pounding of her heartbeat in her ears muffled the

conversation around her as Hilda locked eyes with her worst nightmare. Her stomach lurched as icy fear wrapped around her heart and squeezed, stealing the life from her body.

Valen rose to his feet. "This is the thief?"

Valen kept talking, but Hilda heard no more as her father's eyes widened and then narrowed into furious slits. The air rushed from her lungs, leaving her with a painful clawing feeling in her chest. Yet she still could not draw breath. She had been discovered. He knew she was not dead, that she had run from him.

"Já," Ulf said. "This is the man caught in north passage."

"He killed my boy and three others. Let me take his head now." Kal dug the blade into flesh until blood streamed down his prisoner's neck.

Hilda almost wilted under her father's hateful glare. The dull thud of her heart beating in her ears rose to a deafening crescendo as his gaze held her captive. She couldn't move, couldn't breathe. Her fingers rose to her throat as she fought down the chunks of apple threatening to rise up. And she knew then that her father would never forgive her betrayal.

"The north passage!" Valen roared. "Impossible, it is known only to a few."

"Já. Brother, it is truth. He was caught attempting to exit through the tunnel with gold he had stolen from numerous lodgings."

Hilda sank back in her chair, unable to focus. Though her father's gaze had shifted to Ulf, she still could not move such was the heaviness of her nausea and the roaring in her ears.

Realization lit Valen's face, then his eyes narrowed.

The pieces of apple she had just eaten tried to claw their way back up her throat. Now that the Jarl knew that they had a traitor living amongst the clan, he would not stop until he discovered who endangered his family and people.

"Take his hands," someone shouted from the back of the room.

"Then his head," yelled another.

Valen walked around the table and crossed his arms over his chest, looking every bit the powerful Jarl as he studied the thief. "Now that I know you have an accomplice within my walls, things are making sense. This is not the first time you have stolen from Gottland is it, old man?"

With every word that was spoken Hilda felt her life in Visby slipping further away.

Ulf slammed his hands on the table, making her jump, then spoke through gritted teeth. "You think he stole the gold two years ago?"

Curse the gods, this was like throwing tinder on his smoldering anger. Ulf rarely mentioned it, but she knew he was still furious at himself for failing in his duty to the clan. She knew it tore him up inside that thieves had slipped through his defenses, past his wall, and now it had happened again. The fact that it was through his tunnel made it worse, much worse.

Valen nodded. "With help from someone inside. They used the tunnel to get in and out without being caught last time."

In three steps Ulf was around the table and storming toward her father. "Who told you about the tunnel?" he roared, his fury evident on his handsome features.

Looking nonchalantly past the angry man bearing down on him, her father locked eyes with her once more and his mouth formed a malicious grin.

"You are looking mighty hale for a dead woman, Odell."

Ulf paused mid-step. "Odell? That is not her name. What are you talking about?"

Her father smirked and Ulf's gaze narrowed. Confusion wrinkled his brow as he turned, and his head whipped back and forth between her and her father. "You know my wife?"

His question forced Hilda to her feet. "Ulf," she said quietly, reaching her hand out for her husband as she implored her father with her eyes to stop.

"Wife?"

She swallowed hard, forcing the despair in her throat down as the face that so closely resembled her own twisted into a pleased grin and he laughed.

"Even for you this is good work, Odell. A masterful play."

Hilda stepped forward, her thighs banging against the table and upsetting her cup of mead. "Don't," she begged, though she knew deep down that nothing she said would stop him from destroying her. The cool mead dripped off the table and soaked into her dress. Her stomach roiled, for what had just a few moments ago smelled so sweet, was now as acrid and nauseating as the outhouse on a hot summer's day.

"Hilda?" Ulf asked, frowning at her.

For a few short moments, she memorized the sight of Ulf for she knew that it would be the last time she could look upon him without seeing disdain in his eyes.

"Your wife…Hilda"—her father paused for dramatic affect —"is in truth my daughter, Odell, the best thief I ever trained."

Time slowed to a torturous crawl as Ulf balked and the color drained from his face. "What?"

Biting her lip, Hilda fought to keep from collapsing as her world crumbled around her. She could not take in a proper breath to fill her chest.

"You didn't think she arrived in Visby by chance, did you? Nei. I sent her to find you, to lure you into bed and find a way to get past that wall that you built."

Absently, she picked at her thumb, welcoming the bite of pain as her fingernail tore at the flesh. It seemed like each word that he spoke shook another stone loose until she was left standing in the ruins of her life.

"She was good, Já? The lovesick noble girl distracting the stonemason into spilling his secrets. Spread her legs and caught

you in her trap, she did. We were on our way back to the mainland before you even knew the gold was missing."

"Hilda?" Ulf's voice was hoarse, his pained plea accompanied
by an imploring gaze that broke her heart. "Is this true?"

Though he wanted her to deny it, she could not lie to him
anymore. Accepting that the time for lies was over, she nodded.

"You're his daughter?" Valen said, his tone harsh.

Nodding once more, Hilda wondered what the fearsome Jarl
would do. Would he banish her? Or would she suffer the same
fate as her father and die for her crimes? She dropped her gaze
to the floor, awash with shame. Blood flowed down her thumb,
thick red droplets falling at her feet. She should never have lied
to Ulf. She should have trusted him from the beginning. It
didn't matter which way she looked—she was damned. Now she
was surrounded by lies and twisted truths.

"She faked her death and came back to wed you and take
everything you have. She's no fool, my daughter."

Hilda looked up at her father, then at Ulf, noting how his jaw
hardened and the vein in his neck throbbed.

Ulf remained quiet, and that silence was more deadly and
telling than all the words in the world. He would never forgive
her.

"You are not of a noble family?" Valen asked, his penetrating
gaze searching hers for answers.

Hilda tried to swallow, but her throat was so dry and choked
with too many conflicting emotions. She shook her head, her
voice hoarse. "Nei. I was born an outlaw and raised by my
father."

"You are a thief?" The Jarl looked confused, almost as though
he didn't believe it.

"Nei. I *was* a thief. I am no longer that person." Hilda turned
to point at her pathetic excuse for a father. "He forced me to do
unspeakable things. He has beaten me since I was a small child.
But I could not keep doing them after he robbed you the first

time. I came here because…" She stifled a sob. "For the first time I saw decent people."

"Decent people?" Ulf's voice sounded strangled.

She turned to face him, her heart in her throat.

He shook his head at her. "You lied about everything, even your name."

"I fell in love with you, Ulf. I know what I did was wrong. I just wanted to turn my back on him"— she gestured to her father—"and live with people who were kind and loving."

Ulf pivoted and strode toward the door.

"Ulf, you have seen my scars! They were from him!" she yelled, pointing to her vicious parent.

But Ulf had already turned away, striding quickly to the entry, his big hands curled into fists.

Hilda rushed after him, clutching his arm. "Ulf, I can explain."

With an icy glare that felt like a dagger to her heart, he shook her hand off. "Don't touch me," he growled, then stormed out the door, taking with him any hope she had that all was not lost.

He hated her.

CHAPTER SEVEN

*U*lf's hand tightened on the chisel when the heavy oak door creaked open, letting in a cool blast of night air.

Hilda.

Nobody but his deceitful wife would enter his workshop without knocking. This was his sanctuary, the one place he could escape the demands of his work and lose himself in the joy of carving for pleasure. Before they had met, he'd spent all his spare time in this old cottage with no windows that had once belonged to his teacher, the master stonemason. In the years since the old man had passed, the cottage had tilted dangerously to one side, but the inside remained unchanged, with the metal oil lanterns hanging from wooden beams overhead illuminating the long wooden benches scattered with carving tools, half-finished projects, and a thick layer of crushed dust.

Keeping his back to her, he remained bent over the workbench, his hands moving in calm steady strokes on the picture stone.

"Ulf?" Hilda said, her voice wary.

He stiffened, and refused to acknowledge her, continuing to carve the circular pattern.

"I returned from the hunt two days ago." She'd moved closer, now standing just behind him. He'd always thought her silent steps were those of the graceful poise of a noblewoman, but now he knew better. She had the stealth of a thief.

He grunted. He'd known she was back the moment she was within sight of the wall, but he'd continued sleeping in his workshop, even avoiding mealtimes in the hall to ensure they did not cross paths lest his anger boil over. He didn't want to see her, see anyone. Even whilst she was away, he'd only left his workshop to supervise the new tower construction. How could he face his brother and the rest of the clan when he had failed them? He couldn't. He had slept with the enemy, married her. He just couldn't bear to see the disappointment on their faces. He threw the chisel down in disgust.

Releasing a heavy sigh, Hilda continued. "Valen at least listened to my story. Can you not give me that, Ulf?"

He turned to face her. Gods, he didn't want this, to argue with Hilda, to hear her excuses. But she was stubborn—he should have known she would seek him out eventually.

"Oh, now you want to talk? Speak if you must," he growled, hoping that the firm press of his lips and his glowering countenance would shatter any hopes she had that his temper may have cooled and cause her to make a hasty retreat.

Hilda bit her lip, and for a moment it seemed he had succeeded as shame flashed across her face.

"I know you are angry," she said, then her eyes skimmed over the broad lines of his shoulders and down his muscular arms to where the sleeves of his white shirt were rolled up to the elbows.

"You think..." His blood heated under her admiring perusal, but he arched a brow at her, wiped the dust from his hands, and tossed the cloth aside. He couldn't have her think that looking at him like she wanted to tear his clothes off would change anything.

"You lied to me, about *everything*."

She reached out, her hand sliding down his arm as she spoke. "I lied to you because I was afraid. My fear made me make bad decisions. If you would listen to me, I can try to make you understand."

Ulf scoffed and shook his head in disbelief. Did she really expect him to believe that?

"I never lied about loving you."

Gods, how he wished that were truth. "How do I know? Everything else was a lie." Was every touch, every smile, part of a plot to fool him? It didn't matter what she said, he couldn't trust that any of it was real. "I don't even know you, Hilda, Odell. Whatever your name is."

Hilda winced, her face blanching at his words. "You do know me," she stammered. Inhaling a deep, shaky breath she continued. "Odell is dead. Hilda is who I really am. You know me better than anyone."

Ulf frowned as she closed the distance between them. She was so close that he could see the lighter flecks of green in her emerald eyes and the small scar beneath her eyebrow.

"I did not want to steal, ever, but my father forced me. He..."

"He what?" Ulf snapped, tiring of her attempt to convince him of her innocence. Everyone knew that a child born into the outlaw life was taught to lie, steal, and cheat before they could walk. There was nothing innocent about his outlaw wife.

"He made me steal," she repeated.

Ulf watched her gaze fix in the distance as the memories flooded back.

"I was just three summers, the first time I stole something. Father pushed me under a table at a feast to steal from the pockets of drunk warriors. I was terrified, but even then, I knew not to refuse him. Within a few years he had me climbing through windows to search for gold."

As she spoke, Ulf studied her intently. Though it went against everything he now knew about her, he saw no signs of deceit. Despite himself, he believed her. He had seen her scars, knew that the man who should have protected and loved her had beaten her cruelly. Yet still he could not let her story sway him.

"You had ample time to tell me the truth. There is naught you can say to change that. You knew it was wrong, Hilda."

"I tried to refuse to do it. I promise, I did."

Her plea was so heartful, so earnest, that he wasn't sure if it was truth or if he was falling for her masterful lies, again. Gods, he couldn't even trust his own judgement anymore.

"But if I disobeyed, he would beat me," she continued, speaking so softly that he could barely hear her.

Ulf resisted the urge to pull Hilda into his arms and comfort her. He hated that she had suffered so at the hands of a murderous coward.

Wiping away the tear that rolled down her cheek, she straightened her shoulders. "I know I did wrong. I swear I did not want to steal from you, Ulf. Not long after we first met, I swore to myself I would not do it. I was falling in love with you."

His heart leapt with foolish hope at her declaration, but then she smiled softly at him as though sensing she was wearing him down, and he remembered all the times she had lied to him.

"Yet you stole the gold," he reminded her. Only a fool would fall for her tricks again, and he was no fool.

Looking down shamefully, she wrung her hands. "Já. I went to where Father was camped outside the wall the night before and told him I could not do it. Gods, he was so furious." Her fingers plucked at the corner of where her thumb met her nail.

Ulf felt his brow furrow as he watched her tug at the skin absently. It must hurt, yet she seemed to not notice, to not know she was even doing it. Now that he thought on it, it was a nervous habit she'd had when they first met, one she had overcome. But he'd seen her doing it in the great hall the last time he'd seen her, and now again, both times when speaking of her father. *What did it mean?*

Her eyes lifted to meet his, revealing the depths of her defeat before she even voiced it. "He beat me and then told me that if I didn't open the tunnel, he would use a blade next time."

"So, you did it. You were the traitor."

Releasing a heavy sigh, Hilda nodded. "Afterward, I knew that I had to get away from him, one way or another. He was going to kill me."

"So you left."

"I wish it were that easy. He was never going to just let me go. I waited two months before I got the chance to get away. I threw myself into the flooded river hoping that I would not survive."

A memory flashed in his mind of her telling him that she'd fallen into a river when he'd asked about her torn dress the day she returned. She could have said she'd walked through a blizzard and he would not have cared, so happy was he to see her again. It seemed like the best lies really were close to the truth.

"But you lived."

"I climbed out downstream and I came back to Visby, to you."

"Why? Why did you come back?"

"I love you. I could not go back to that life, to being beaten. You showed me that life could be good, that people could be good. I fell in love with you."

"Lies." Even as he said it the insult tasted bitter on his tongue. Despite all Hilda's lies, he believed that she loved him. That could not be faked, even by the best actress. Could it? Shaking off the disturbing thought, he continued. "Because of your lies I have failed twice to protect Visby, failed at my duty."

Hilda flinched. "I am so sorry."

"You brought them through the tunnel, Hilda. The tunnel *I built* to protect my family, my clan."

Her face flushed red as she bit down on her lip and hung her head.

A pang of guilt hit as she wilted before his eyes, but he forged on, recounting the wreckage she had caused. "Our marriage was a lie. I thought I married a noblewoman. You are an outlaw, a thief." He fairly spat the last words at her, so disgusted was he with himself for falling for her ruse.

Her back went ramrod straight and she glared at him. "I am not a thief. I *was* a thief. My father knows how to twist words, to manipulate people. It is why the outlaws follow him. They will soon come to free him, for they will never abandon their leader. If you believe anything about what I say, you must believe this."

"I do not believe either of you," he said, deciding to double the watch anyway.

"Do you even know how hard it was to speak of this, for me to show you my scars?" Stepping forward, she raised a hand and poked him in the chest hard. "You told me there was nothing I could tell you that would change how you felt about me. You promised, Ulf."

Pushing her hand away, he pinned her with a cold stare. "Já, but I never thought it would be that you are an outlaw. That promise was made to a woman that does not exist." His Hilda was gone, replaced by a stranger. "I can never look at you the same way again."

"I have suffered enough—I refuse to let him continue to hurt me. So now that you know the truth your word means nothing?"

"That is not fair, Hilda." Curse her for being right. He *had* asked her to trust him and given her his word. His stomach revolted, his evening meal rising up in his throat. What man did not keep his word?

"Don't do this, Hilda!" He slammed his hand down on the bench. "This can never work."

"Are you… Do you mean our marriage…" He watched as the blood drained from her face. "Are you saying that our marriage is over?" she whispered.

"Mayhap," he said, and shrugged.

She looked down and wrung her hands. Surely, she had to have known that there was no coming back from this, that he could not trust her and now she knew she could not trust him either. What was a marriage without trust?

"Just go," he said, squaring his shoulders.

"Ulf. I need to tell you—"

"Gods, Hilda. Just leave." He couldn't bear a long painful drawn out goodbye. She needed to go, just leave and not look back.

Placing her hands on her hips, Hilda jutted her chin defiantly. "You spoke of seeing us with children and grandchildren…"

"Son of Loki! What does that have to do with anything?" He was angry now. Why could she not just let it go? Let him go?

"I am with child." The words were uttered with the same deadly calm as an arrow whistling through the woods to meet its target.

A child? His child? His eyes narrowed and an icy warning clawed at his insides. Lies. More lies. How dare she use their desire for a child against him!

"Ulf—"

"Get out," he roared, unable to contain the force of his fury.

Hilda gasped, tears pooling in her eyes before her hand fell to cradle her stomach and she turned from him.

The truth hit him like lightning hitting water, sending sparks throughout his entire body. Now that he looked more closely, she was rounder, her body lusher, her stomach no longer flat. She *was* with child. He stepped forward with one arm outstretched, overcome with the instinct to protect her, protect his child.

But she was gone, leaving the old wooden door creaking on its hinges as she fled into the darkness.

CHAPTER EIGHT

ULF

The night was dark and silent but for the soft hoot of a watchful owl nestled in the highest branches of an oak tree. Ulf watched Hilda climb the steps to the tower where he stood watch over the harbor.

The moonlight caressed the gentle curve where her neck met her shoulder and the softness of her cheek, then their eyes met and everything else melted away.

In the two days since she'd come to his workshop, he'd almost convinced himself that what he felt for her was a lie, but at that moment he knew he was just fooling himself. No matter what she had done, his feelings for Hilda were, despite being complicated, real. Thief, outlaw, noble. Confused as he was about who she was, he still loved her. Somehow knowing that was even worse. He had to give her up and he knew that losing her would destroy him.

"What are you doing here, Hilda?" he said from where he stood in the shadows.

"You have not been home in days. We must talk."

"I have naught to say to you."

"Then do not speak." Leveling him with a hard stare and

then crossing her arms, she continued. "I think we need to divorce." There was a sadness in her eyes, but also a resignation that made him want to go to battle for her, for them.

"Divorce?" The word tasted bitter on his tongue.

"You needn't avoid me all the time. I know I have ruined everything. Bring Valen to the cottage tomorrow and you can begin the declarations for divorce. You will be free to marry again." Her bottom lip trembled as she spoke those last words, her eyes filling with tears.

Him, take another wife? Or have another family, while she and the baby would be forced to live the outlaw life? Gods, no. He did not want that for her or their child, but it would be the likely outcome if they divorced. He reached for her as she turned to leave, attempting to escape before he saw her tears.

"There is no point continuing like this, Ulf. I would not keep you in a marriage you do not want."

A marriage he did not want. He wasn't even sure he knew what he wanted, but he knew what felt wrong. "Yesterday I would have agreed with you, but now I am not so sure I can let you go."

She eyed him warily, clearly not believing his change of heart. "I know it is my own fault, but I cannot raise a child in a home with a man that does not trust me."

"I don't know how to fix this, but I do not want that either."

"So now you believe I am with child?"

"I knew when you told me. I just was too angry to admit it. Then Ola told me you had been to see her to get something to settle your stomach in the mornings because the child made you ill." He neglected to mention that the healer had smacked him in the back of the head and ranted at him about his foolishness.

Her honey-brown eyes shot daggers at him. "See, I am right to ask for a divorce. You trust someone else, but not me. How could you think I would lie about that, about our child?" Her voice shook, and for a moment her pain was evident in the thin line of her lips and her tense features before she regained control. "Living in a home where parents are at war is not good for any child. I want a calm and loving home for my child."

Running a hand through his hair, he nodded in agreement. Her anger was justified—he had been shocked and behaved like an ass. "I want that too."

Tilting her head, Hilda looked at him curiously. "Do you even think that is possible? Or is our marriage too broken?"

As much as Ulf wanted to give the answer she wanted to hear, he couldn't. "I don't know, Hilda. I do not know how to fix this. I cannot even ask my parents or Valen for advice as they are all happily married. But if it is broken, then I have to believe that it can be fixed."

"What will it take for you to trust me again? If you have your men watch me, will that help?"

"Mayhap…" *What was she suggesting?*

"Then do it."

"You want me to have you followed?" Not trusting her and having her followed seemed like an odd way to find his way back to trusting her.

Hilda nodded, a determined glint in her eye. "I will do anything to prove that you can trust me. Let me show you."

Ulf nodded in agreement. "Very well. Pétr will follow you for a while."

"Good. You will see that I have no more secrets to hide. You know that the outlaws my father travels with will come for him?"

Ulf stiffened at the mention of her father. "They'll not get him. Nobody will get at Ubbi Tannrsson until Valen has ruled on his crimes."

"Mayhap, but be careful. Though few in number, they are dangerous. Anyone caught in their way, even women and children, will be cut down."

"Why do you tell me this?"

"I decided where my loyalties lay on the day we wed, Ulf. I know you do not believe it yet, but this is my clan too, my people. I do not want anyone to get hurt." Stretching up, she placed her lips on his and kissed him, hesitantly.

He stiffened, his lips remaining as hard and guarded as his heart.

A weary sigh escaped her. "If you do not want divorce, then I would have a true marriage and share a bed." Squaring her shoulders, she backed away. "This time it will be different between us. I will hide *nothing* from you," she said, raising an eyebrow.

His blood heated at the suggestive innuendo.

"I will be different, Ulf."

A cool spring breeze sent a shiver up his spine as he took in the steely determination in her eyes before she turned and walked away. Resting his hands on the rough stone, Ulf looked out at the moonlight shimmering across the sea, wondering if he'd just made another foolish mistake.

Could he ever trust a thief?

CHAPTER NINE

ULF

"*U*lf?"

"Já." Setting down his chisel beside the runestone he'd been working on all afternoon, Ulf turned to watch Pétr step hesitantly into his workshop.

The apprentice who'd been watching Hilda loped toward him with the gangly awkwardness of a boy not yet a man, his mop of dark hair flopping wildly.

"What is it, Pétr?" he asked, and sensing no urgency to the boy's arrival, returned to his carving.

His curiosity obvious, the youth's gaze fell to the large picture stone Ulf had been working on the last few days. "I followed Hilda outside the wall today," he said.

Ulf's head snapped up and he eyed the boy with interest. What was Hilda doing beyond the wall? "Did she meet with someone?"

"Nei." Pétr's gaze never left the picture stone on the bench, his eyes studying with interest the intricate design.

Ulf ran his thumb over the carved figure of Óðinn, satisfied at the smooth surface. He carved many of these picture stones each year, so that families could erect them in memory of those they had lost. He would soon pass on the knowledge and tradition to Pétr. Ulf looked at the boy and raised an eyebrow. Receiving no response, he huffed his impatience.

The boy's eyes rose to meet his, and then he could not get the words out fast enough. "She took her bow and quiver, so I thought she was going hunting. But she just wandered around for hours picking smultron. I swear she must have enough to make jam."

Ulf stilled at the mention of the wild strawberries that were his favorite. His mouth watered just thinking about the intense burst of flavor exploding in his mouth and Hilda's strawberry pies. She had pestered his mother for her recipe, and then learned to make the strawberry pies, just for him.

"What do you think she is doing with all those berries?" Pétr asked.

Ulf couldn't help the smile curving up the corners of his mouth. He knew exactly why she had picked smultron when she'd known the boy was watching and would report back to him. It was a message—she was offering his favorite pie to entice him home. Could he go home?

"Tell me, has Hilda done naught but work and stay close to home these last weeks?" he asked.

"Já. She goes nowhere. It is tiresome watching her do naught. Can one of the other boys watch her now? I want to train with the men."

Ulf crossed his arms over his chest and stared down his nose at his apprentice. "Are you saying that there is something more important than watching over and protecting my wife?"

Pétr shook his head hastily. "Nei. Nei. It is an honor. I will watch her carefully for you."

"Já. I knew you were the right man for the job. You may go. I will watch over Hilda until you arrive in the morning."

A big grin split the boy's face. "Thanks, Ulf," he said, and then raced out the door as though worried Ulf would change his mind.

Walking to the cot where he'd been sleeping these past few weeks, Ulf threw his clothes into his bag and headed for the door. It was time to return to his wife and his bed. Winding his way through town, he made his way to the bustling market where stallholders stood outside their stands chatting in the late afternoon dappled light as harried mothers lugging baskets of produce chased down wayward children.

"Well met, Una," he said, greeting the wife of one of his father's retired warriors.

"Ulf, it has been a while since I have seen you." She smiled up at him, her silver hair and the deep lines at the corners of her eyes not matching the youthful sparkle in her pale blue eyes. "How is the new tower construction coming along?"

He couldn't help but grin back at her. "It is good. Should be done by winter."

"I am sure the men will be happy for the shelter from the cold. Do you need something?"

"Já. Some cinnamon."

"Is Hilda making pies?"

He shrugged casually, feigning indifference. "Mayhap."

Una's shrewd gaze considered him for a few moments. "I heard that Hilda lied about her past."

Gods, he did not want to talk about this. "Já."

Scooping cinnamon into a small pouch, she continued. "Never seen a woman more in love than that one. It is good you have not given up on her."

"It is?" The words burst forth before he could contain them. He'd never thought for a moment that anyone would think that he should stay married to Hilda. He'd half expected the clan to march to his home and demand that she be banished for being a traitor and a thief. Mayhap that was why Valen had delayed in passing judgement on her and her father? Maybe he knew that with a little time tempers would cool.

Una patted him gently on the shoulder. "Marriage is about not giving up on the other person, Ulf. Even when we discover their faults." She pressed the small leather pouch into his hand.

"Thanks, Una." Fishing a coin from his pocket, he tossed it to her and turned for home.

"You enjoy those pies now," Una called out, her cheerful chuckle making him shake his head.

~

The sweet aroma of stewed berries assaulted his nostrils as Ulf stepped inside the cottage and kicked off his boots near the door.

Hilda lifted the pot from the fire and moved to hang it on the metal hook over the counter to cool, her eyes following his every move but saying nothing as he placed his bag inside their bedchamber.

"I went to the market," he said, breaking the awkward silence as he walked to where she stood.

She looked up at him, her eyes filled with wary hope. "You did?"

"Já." He pulled the small pouch of cinnamon from his pocket and placed it on the counter. "For the pies."

She untied the pouch, smiling when the smell of cinnamon wafted out. "Does this mean…?" She paused, her eyes returning to his, the unspoken question heavy between them.

"I don't want a divorce, Hilda."

Her eyes filled with tears. "Neither do I."

He pulled her into his arms, his hand caressing her head soothingly as she cried into his chest. "I don't know how we make this work, but I want to try. I want us to be a family."

She pulled back, brushed the tears from her cheeks, and looked up at him. "Me too. Are you going to sleep here now?"

Ulf smiled at her, mischief lighting his eyes. "If you are making strawberry pies."

The sound of her laughter warmed his heart. Then she turned and motioned at the pot hanging to cool. "There will be no pie until morning. You shall have to wait."

Dipping his head, Ulf licked behind her ear and scraped his teeth across her earlobe.

"Then I shall have to feast on you instead."

~

*H*ilda's heart skipped a beat as Ulf trailed kisses down her neck, then raced with delight as he swept her into his arms and strode into their chamber.

"Gods, I want you," he said as he placed her on her feet.

Blessed Freya, when he spoke in that low husky rumble heat flared between her thighs.

"I want you too," she said, her fingers trembling as she unfastened the brooches that held her apron dress in place and let it fall to the floor. Not giving herself time to hesitate, she pulled her underdress over her head and tossed it aside.

"Gods, you are so beautiful." Her husband's eyes were lit with desire as he spoke, and then he pulled his shirt over his head and she lost the ability to breathe. With the light from the lanterns in the kitchen hitting his sculpted chest, he looked like he was bathed in gold, like he was a god, like Óðinn himself.

Though the fear had come rushing back as she stood there in naught but her shift, his words and the fire in his eyes gave her the strength to continue. And so, she lifted the skirts of her shift and pulled it over her head, baring herself to him.

His hastily removed clothes were tossed into a pile on the floor.

His fingers brushed over the scars on her stomach, softly, reverently. Giving her the courage to reach up and trace her fingers over the stubble on his angular jaw. "I love you, Ulf. I never meant to hurt you."

Ulf held her gaze, his eyes searing right through her. "I love you too." His body pressed against hers, guiding her to lay on the bed and then hovering over her before he dipped his head and claimed her lips in a tender kiss.

Wrapping an arm around his neck, she pulled him down and kissed him back. He was hot, and hard, and hers. Her heart sang. He loved her, despite everything, he loved her.

Ulf pulled away and moved to kiss down her neck and across her chest, his tongue teasing at her nipple before he suckled.

She reached up, gripping the carved wooden headboard, made by her husband in one of his rare forays into shaping wood, not stone. She could not count the number of times she had gripped the timber to brace herself in the throes of their lovemaking. Somehow, the sensation of the smooth timber beneath her fingers contrasted with her husband's dominant ardor always sent her hurtling into bliss.

As though reading her thoughts, the slick wet heat of Ulf's lips clamped down on her other nipple making her arch into his touch.

"More," she whimpered. Gods, she wanted so much more. She looked up at him, begging him with her eyes for the pleasure she knew only his steely manhood could provide.

He smiled down at her, his blue eyes glowing with hunger.

Her heart thudded in her chest, for she knew what was to come. He would touch her, tease her, drive her wild with need and make her beg before he took her.

His lips were warm and soft as he kissed her slowly, as though savoring the taste of her. The rough brush of calloused hand sliding up her thigh reminded her that he was a strong rugged man with the strength to take her, yet she knew he would only bring her pleasure with his rough loving.

He deepened the kiss as the fabric moved upward, his mouth moving with an urgent savage intensity that left her reeling.

"Look at me."

Pulling away, she looked at where they were almost joined, before her gaze rose to meet his. "I would take naught that you do not wish to give. If we join, I would have it be as I always wished, neither of us holding back, two becoming one," she said.

Ulf answered her with a slow thrust that impaled her on his length.

"You cannot handle all of me, wife," he growled.

A wry smile curved her lips as she rocked her hips. "Try me." She felt as though the shy and reserved persona she had hidden behind had fallen away with the last of her clothing and the end of her deceit.

Eyes locked, Ulf gripped her firm bottom and lifted, sliding her off all but the very tip of him.

Hilda whimpered, bereft at the loss of his hard rod.

Dipping his head, Ulf swirled his tongue around the rosy nipple, his lips furling in satisfaction as it tightened into a bud. He took it in his warm mouth and suckled, then the other one, going back and forth, devouring her. His hunger was insatiable.

"More," she begged, her thighs clamped around his hips holding him firmly in place as her eyes closed and her head fell back.

Releasing her nipple, he rolled until she was atop him and slowly eased her down on his throbbing staff, encouraging her to ride him.

Soon their bodies moved in a sensual rhythm. She held his broad shoulders as she rose up and slammed down on him with a delicious friction that she could tell made him eager to spill himself inside her.

"Kiss me," she demanded, and cupped his face and drew him

into a kiss that quickly moved from teasingly languid to needy and frantic.

Hands cupped, grasped, and fingers tweaked. Hips rose and fell in an exquisite harmony, until mouths fused, and they shuddered in unison and soared as one.

Breathless and replete, Hilda lay beside Ulf, his hands caressing the curve of her waist and hips before he pulled a fur over them to ward off the cool night air. She had never felt so close to him as this moment. That he was still having her watched and did not trust her yet weighed on her, but now there was hope. Hope that somehow they would find their way.

CHAPTER TEN

ULF

"Where is she?" Ulf asked, storming toward where Pétr stood beside the garden plot. He wanted to believe Hilda would not betray him again, but he was not foolish enough to let it happen a third time. And now Pétr had sent for him in the middle of the day.

"This way."

Ulf followed his apprentice through the garden, his mood sinking with every step. The boy would not have sent for him if something wasn't very wrong. This past week everything with Hilda had been wonderful. Now that everything had been laid bare between them, there was new depth to their closeness and feelings for each other. They had barely left their home, choosing not to stray too far from their bedchamber now that they could make love unfettered. And make love they did, day and night, with wild abandon.

Pétr halted behind the young spruce tree near the well and peered around. "She's been standing there for a long time," he whispered, then ducked back into hiding.

Ulf parted the tips of the green foliage and searched for his wife.

Her red hair shone like a beacon in the sunlight as she stood before the door that led into the prisoner cells that were all empty bar the one that held her father. She shuffled back and forth, her lips moving as she muttered to herself, looking uncertain.

Don't do it. He watched with bated breath as she wrestled a few moments longer with her decision.

She turned and looked around furtively before slipping through the doorway that led to the prisoners' cells, leaving the door ajar behind her.

His stomach dropped. He had trusted her, even moved back into their home, and barely a week later she was betraying him yet again. Waving off Pétr, he crossed the grassy lawn and slipped through the doorway, following her into the darkness, all the while berating himself. There could only be one reason she was here, to help her father escape. He had been so sure he could trust her this time, but he couldn't. Could he?

The inky blackness and comforting press of cool stone against his back brought him back to reality. Using the stone wall for shelter, he peered around the corner.

Hilda stood outside her father's cell. Even now, she looked as though she were summoning her strength for what was to come.

He stood in the utter silence waiting to see what she would do. Something was not right. If she had come to free her father, she would have done it quickly, not stood outside debating it. These were not the actions of a thief, but of a woman wrestling with a dilemma. *What was she doing?*

Sighing heavily, Hilda spoke, her voice a low whisper.

As the metal chink of keys echoed around him, his heart turned to stone.

Her father replied, their hushed voices rolling up the corridor like a roll of deep thunder. He couldn't hear what was being said, but it did not matter. Her actions screamed betrayal

—she had come here alone, with the keys, and now they were making plans for escape.

Squeezing his eyes closed, Ulf lay his forehead against the wall. He would never understand why she had made such a decision. He had thought that she was finally honest with him, but it had been just another ploy to get him to lower his defenses.

CHAPTER ELEVEN

"*H*ilda. What took so long, girl?"

As soon as she heard the bitter raspy tone of his voice, Hilda wondered if she had made a terrible mistake. Yet another terrible nightmare last eve had brought her here. She'd woken in a cold sweat, paralyzed by fear, and known that she could not continue like that for the rest of her life. It didn't matter if Ulf trusted or forgave her, or even if she forgave herself—until she faced the fear that was haunting her, she would never be free. And she wanted that, she wanted to be free, to rest easy at night and live a happy life. She could not bring this darkness into her life with Ulf or it would destroy them both, so she had come here to face him, to banish it.

"I had to steal the key," she said, her voice croaking as she forced out the words. Gods, how she'd hated herself for taking the key from Ulf's bag that morning, but she needed them to get through the front door. For a brief moment she had considered asking Ulf to bring her here, but she knew that having him here would not work. The problem that caused the nightmares was in her mind and to overcome it she needed to face her fears alone to know that *she* could defeat them. She would not let Ulf or anyone else steal that victory from her.

"Open the door then. Let's go," he said, approaching the bars, and then looking left then right for any guards.

"Nei." She fingered the keys absently, her eyes locked on his. "Nei?"

"I am not opening it. That is not why I have come." Even she was surprised at the edge of steel in her voice.

"What did you say?" her father said, turning his good ear to the bars so as to hear her better. He was almost deaf in one ear after a particularly bad drunken brawl a few summers past.

Hilda stepped closer to repeat herself louder.

"I still cannot hear you," he said.

"I-I," she stammered, before recovering and then continuing in a stronger voice. "I am not releasing you. I am married now. My place is here with my husband."

Suddenly, his hand darted out and gripped the fabric of her dress, yanking her into the bars, hard.

Dazed, Hilda swayed on her feet as he snatched the key from her hand. Before she had even recovered, he had unlocked the cell door and was standing before her in the corridor.

"Acting like a noble woman does not make you one, Odell. Your place is with me," he sneered.

Cringing, she backed away, desperate to get beyond reaching distance. "Father, let me go. I cannot live that life anymore."

She barely heard the dull thud of his fist hitting her jaw as her head snapped to the side. Pain sparked, hot and sharp. Gods, she had forgotten how much it hurt to be hit, the pain, the lights, the darkness threatening at the edges of her vision. Her time with Ulf had made her weak to the onslaught of physical pain that she had once taken with the same ease as a regularly beaten hound.

"A year ago, I would never have gotten the keys from you. Being here, living with these people has made you weak. You are not the same thief." His hand yanked hard on her hair until her eyes watered. "You'll do as you're told, Odell."

The stinging burning pain of hair being ripped from her scalp snapped her mind to utter clarity. There was more at stake than just her. She had to protect the life growing inside her from him. She would not allow her child to suffer at this man's hands too. Ignoring the stinging of her scalp, Hilda looked up into his wild eyes. She stilled at the calculating evil reflected back at her. He fed off of her fear and as long as she gave it to him this would never be over. Glaring back, she spat out the words that would destroy his power over her.

"My name is Hilda. I would rather die than go back to being Odell."

His hand wrapped around her throat, crushing painfully until she could not breathe. "Your husband controls the wall defense. He must die for us to escape," he growled, as though she had not spoken.

Her eyes felt like they were bulging out of their sockets, but she did not claw at his hand around her throat.

"You will kill him." Slowly, his fingers relaxed, and then he shoved her away.

Gasping, Hilda fought back the bile threatening to rise in her throat.

"It will be easier to leave after dark. You will kill him and then meet me at the tunnel."

Kill Ulf? Her entire being revolted against the thought. She was no murderer. She shook her head vehemently.

"I will never hurt him."

"You will," he hissed. He stepped forward, raising clenched fists in an attempt to regain control over her.

Hilda backed away, inching toward the open door. Coming here was a terrible mistake. She would never be safe as long as her father lived, she knew that now. She was not leaving Visby, ever. This was her home, her people. For the first time in her life she felt loved, felt safe. She would not give that up.

"I will not kill the man I love. Nothing you say or do will change that." As shock and understanding registered on his face she finally saw behind his evil façade. He was an aging man desperately clinging to the last remnants of his fading power with the outlaws, before he was overthrown by a younger, more dangerous man. He was nothing, a nobody who would disappear from the world without leaving his mark. That is why he wanted her back, because without her to continue his lawless legacy he would be forgotten. She held the power to wipe him from existence, and that was exactly what she was going to do. She was going to live a happy life with Ulf and ensure that nobody heard tales of Ubbi Tannrsson the thief.

"You are a sad, pathetic old man," she said, and laughed because she knew in that moment that she was finally free of him.

A heartbeat later, he lunged for her, his hand snagging on her dress and pulling her to the floor as his face loomed overhead like a dark threatening cloud.

Heart in her throat, Hilda waited for the inevitable pain. She had never seen him so angry. He would not stop this time. This is where her life would end, on the cold hard floor of a cell whilst he made his escape. Men like him always found a way to slither back under a rock and hide until they were strong enough to find another victim to torment.

At the first blow she saw stars, the back of her head thudding against the stone floor. Wetness seeped into her hair, a cold emptiness filling her on the inside as he hit her in the face. Then she fought back, bucking and kicking and clawing at him. She would not lie down and die. She would not let him steal her child from her.

Her nails dug into his soft flesh and drew blood.

She would not be his victim, not now, not ever again.

CHAPTER TWELVE

*L*eaping though the door, Ulf pulled Ubbi Tannrsson off Hilda and threw him into the metal bars of the cell.

"What in Hel?" he roared at the sight of his wife's bruised face and swollen eye.

Turning as Hilda's father leapt to his feet, Ulf glared at the man and roared. "Did you hurt her?"

"She needed a lesson on where her loyalties lie."

The corridor was not wide, but there was enough room to teach this coward a lesson in manners. "You will never touch my wife again," he hissed.

"Your wife? Your wife came and released me so we could escape. Why are you protecting her?"

Ulf glanced back and forth between Hilda and her father. "Did you release him?"

She shook her head. "Nei. I did take your keys, but—"

"She will always choose her blood, boy. Girl knows her family."

Ulf glanced at where Hilda stood, tears rolling down her face, her fingers picking at that blasted thumb again. A habit she only did when she was afraid, when she spoke of her father. *Lies.*

The man was a liar, just like she'd said. Ulf recognized the scheming cruelty in the eyes of the man before him, knew now that everything Hilda had told him was truth. She had suffered greatly at this man's hands and done what she must to survive.

"You are a liar. But it is true that Hilda knows her family. I am her family."

"You would have her even after she betrayed you?" Ubbi Tannrsson shook his head in disgust.

"I would." He spoke without hesitation and knew in his gut that it was truth. Now he believed that he was her family, that he and their baby were the family she had chosen.

"She is a traitor to her blood. She will die for her betrayal," her father spat, his voice dripping with unleashed hatred, and then he leapt toward Hilda.

Ulf lost all reason. He heard naught but the dull thud of his fists hitting flesh, until the thick wet blood coating his knuckles and seeping between his fingers broke through the haze.

"Ulf," Hilda whimpered, drawing his gaze to where she stood, one hand cradling her stomach, the other wiping the blood from her face. *How badly was she hurt?*

The man below him bucked his hips and yanked on his left arm, throwing him off-balance and tossing him off.

The moment he hit the floor Ulf rolled and jumped to his feet. He had to protect Hilda and his child.

Ubbi Tannrsson wiped the blood from his nose and spat on the floor. "You'll regret that when I am done with you."

Glowering, they circled each other warily.

"Not even on your best day, *old man*," Ulf taunted and struck out with a balled fist.

The man ducked and smirked at Ulf. "I've bested better than you, boy."

"Only the worst kind of coward beats on a child." He'd hoped that the insult would cause the man to lose his temper and make a mistake, but Ubbi just shrugged and tossed out an equally harsh blow.

"She's as useless as her mother. I should've killed her that night too."

Hilda gave a strangled cry.

"You killed her mother?" The man did not have an honorable bone in his body. Killed his own wife and then beat on an innocent child.

"Bitch was going to leave me. I cut her up good."

"Nei!"

Ulf's gaze flicked to Hilda for a mere moment, knowing that her heart was breaking. In the moment of his distraction, he felt the quick jerk of his dagger being lifted from his waist and quickly sidestepped, but the blade bit into his left shoulder, slicing through his flesh. He barely registered the pain—it was a trifling wound compared to those he had suffered on the battlefield.

"After you, she's next." Ubbi struck out with the blade.

Ulf grunted as the blade struck him in the arm and stumbled backward pressing a hand over the gushing wound. It was long past time for this to be over.

～

*H*ilda watched in horror as her father moved in for the death blow now that he had Ulf at a disadvantage. His face constricted in a gleeful mask that made her stomach heave.

One bone crunching punch later, Ulf was straddling her father, his powerful thighs holding him in place.

Though her father lashed out and used all manner of underhanded tricks, Ulf restrained him with casual ease and then lifted him to his feet.

"What is this?" asked the stout warrior rushing toward them with two others not far behind. "We heard shouting."

Hilda sagged against the wall, welcoming the cold press of stone at her back as they moved past her. She looked down at her hands, shaking uncontrollably. She was cold, so cold.

"Tannrsson is just causing some trouble. Lock him back in his cell and set a watch until Valen calls for him," she heard Ulf order, and then the grunting as he handed over the bucking man to his warriors.

"Daughter!" Her father's tone was earnest, pleading.

Hilda's eyes snapped up to meet his.

"You are handing me over to my death, Odell. There is no way the Jarl will let me live."

Hilda froze, an icy chill settling over her. She turned to face him, overcome by pity as she took in the calculating look in his eyes. Stepping forward she shook her head at him.

"You will never change, Father. That is why you will face your fate alone."

He kicked out, struggling in the arms of his captors, enraged that he could no longer control or hurt her with fists or words. He was going to die, and he knew it.

Death was a harsh sentence, but in his case, one she could not fault. Left alive, he would continue to steal and murder any who would defy him. Her father was a monster of the worst kind, and the world would be better off without him.

Then Ulf's towering presence was beside her, his arm wrapping around her waist and pulling her against his warm chest. "It is your own doing, old man. You could have chosen another path, just as my wife has. I will rest easy knowing that you will never hurt my woman or my child, again."

Gentle hands led her down the corridor, and by the time Hilda stood out in the dappled afternoon sunshine, the heavy weight of her past had lifted. She closed her eyes and tipped her face up to the sun, basking in the warmth and enjoying the calm peacefulness she felt within.

"Are you well? Let me hold you." His strong arms surrounded her, and she was pulled back against a hard chest.

She relaxed. "Já. I am well."

"I don't know how you survived him. I see now how he manipulates words, just like you said he would."

Turning in his arms, Hilda looked up into his handsome face. "You believed me."

His expression softened. "Já. I knew that you would never release a man you feared would hurt you, hurt our child." His hand cupped her chin, his thumb brushing over her cheek gently. "Why did you go there, Hilda? You were hurt."

"Bruises that will fade with time. I needed to face him to banish him from my dreams."

Understanding flashed in his blue eyes. "I would have come with you."

"I know. But I needed to do it alone."

Dipping his head, Ulf brushed his lips across hers and then pulled back, looking down at her proudly. "You are so brave. Now I understand why you have bad dreams, and I hope they will not continue."

"They won't." In her heart she knew it to be true. She had banished her fear in that dark corridor, forever.

"He is right, you know. He will die. Valen will have no option but to sentence him to death for his crimes."

Sighing heavily, Hilda slid her arms up Ulf's chest and around his neck. "I know."

"Can you handle that?"

She was suddenly exhausted. "It was his fate. He deserves no mercy."

"We can go if you need to see it done. I will be there, whatever you decide."

"I do not need to see it. I came here to face my fear and overcome my past. It is done."

"He can never hurt you again. You are free now, love."

Tugging gently, she pulled his head down to hers. "Já. I am," she whispered, and then kissed him with the slow, thoughtful tenderness of a woman loving her husband.

CHAPTER THIRTEEN

Hilda snuggled down into the crook of Ulf's arm and pulled the furs over their naked bodies. Laying her hand on his sweaty chest, she breathed in the delicious smell of him. Blessed Freya, she loved this man.

"I am worn out, woman."

A burst of laughter escaped her. "I am glad you pulled me away from the feast early." Sliding her leg between his, she looked up at her husband and smiled, marvelling at how her life had changed in just a few short days. Ulf had sheltered her that day, rushing her home and then dealing with Valen and all of the ensuing questions. Then the Jarl had sent out scouts to chase off the band of outlaws to the mainland, vowing there would be swift retribution should they ever return.

Ulf pressed a kiss to her forehead. "I held out until Valen was done speaking."

"Barely," she said, and laughed.

"I would never steal that moment from you, love. Even if I was picturing you naked the whole time."

"Stop it." She whacked him on the chest. "It was nice that he did that," she mused, her heart swelling at the memory of Valen telling the clan what her father had done to her.

"*She has a new family now,*" he had said, looking at her affectionately. "*She is one of us, and soon to be mother to another Eriksson, my niece or nephew.*"

The cheers of the crowd had been deafening in their approval.

"He is too kind. You all are."

Ulf rose up over her, his arm muscles rippling as he settled between her legs. His blue eyes softened with affection as he spoke. "We all deserve a second chance, love. You have suffered enough for ten lifetimes…"

She shuddered as he shuffled down and pressed tender kisses over the scars on her stomach.

"Now you will know peace as a mother and a wife."

"I am a thief—"

"You are my everything," he said, cutting her off.

"I am?" Wrapping her arms around his neck Hilda pulled him down and pressed her mouth to his in a slow and hungry kiss.

Ulf's blue eyes twinkled when he finally pulled back and looked down at her.

"Já. Little thief, you have stolen my heart."

AFTERWORD

Thank you so much for reading Ulf and Hilda's story. I hope you had a wonderful time with them. Authors love reviews. If you enjoyed this book, please consider leaving a review at your place of purchase.

Would you like to hear about my latest news and releases? If so, then sign up for my newsletter at www.reethornton.com

If you enjoyed Viking Betrayed, you'll love the other Viking Hearts novellas. Keep reading for a sneak peek!

BELOVED VIKING

The shield-maiden must marry...

Heir to her father's Jarldom, Rúna Isaksson will soon ascend to replace him as leader, but first she must marry a warrior from another clan to form a powerful alliance. When her father creates a contest to determine the strongest suitor, Rúna demands to compete as well—if she wins, she can choose her own husband. However, she's shocked to discover that her first love is amongst the competitors, the man who abandoned her without looking back. She must not let him win.

A Viking warrior haunted by a dark past...

Jorvan Eriksson has returned from seeking his fortune to claim his childhood sweetheart, but the girl he left behind has become a battle-hardened shield-maiden with no intention of forgiving him. Jorvan has changed too—he now fights a darkness that lurks in his own mind. Somehow, he must conquer his demons to out-manoeuvre the other suitors and win the Viking games for Rúna's hand. Though victory alone will never be enough. He won't settle for anything less than reclaiming the future Jarl's heart.

FORBIDDEN VIKING

An Arabian Princess tastes freedom...

When Samara Abbasid's ship is attacked she throws herself overboard and seeks refuge in the Viking Jarldom of Gottland. Claiming to be merely a scribe, she temporarily escapes her life of duty and expectation, and is free to sample the Vikings ways. She finds them as seductive as the strong Jarl, Valen. However, if Valen discovers her royal status he could use her as leverage in his trade negotiations with her father, the powerful Caliph. Worse, she must soon return to the royal court and her upcoming arranged marriage. But once she's tasted forbidden pleasure will she be able to return to a life of duty...?

A Jarl bound by duty...

The most powerful Viking clans are assembling on the isle of Gottland to celebrate Valen Eriksson's ascension to Jarl. So Valen is furious to discover rogue Vikings have raided in his territory. Now he must serve swift justice and protect the mysterious survivor until he can return her the Abbasid Caliph. The last thing he needs is to be tempted by the alluring scribe, not when he's sworn to choose a bride from an allied Viking clan. Duty to his clan has always been first and foremost, yet his heart yearns...

WINTER VIKING

A Viking queen on the run...

Widow Ásta Helgesen's husband died years ago in a brutal attack that cost her everything she loved. For four years, she has lived as Ásta Oleander, hiding in plain sight as she mourns her husband. The one time she took a man to her furs, the crushing guilt overwhelmed her brief need to move on and she vowed Dànel would be the last. Now the maniacal King who killed her husband has discovered she's alive and is determined to make her his bride. He's dangerous, powerful and will stop at nothing to get what he wants. Forced to flee, Ásta journeys to the bitterly cold northlands to seek sanctuary in the isolated lands of a man she bedded once, and then rejected. Will he protect her from a murderer? Or has she made a terrible mistake?

A warrior with a painful past...

Following the death of his brother, Dànel Kvitfjell has returned to the Sami northlands to take over the shipping fleet that supports the family village. Yet everything reminds him of the tragedy that led to his childhood banishment and he realises that, after more than a decade fostered with Vikings, his family now feel more like strangers. All he wants is to fulfill his duty to his people and return to life with his Viking comrades, but the unexpected arrival of Ásta and her dangerous secrets jeopardizes everything. Why has the woman who rejected his affections sought him out? Forced to flee deep into the wilderness with Ásta, Dànel must confront the painful past that haunts him. Can he protect Ásta from both the man hunting her and the harsh winter land where one mistake can steal those you love?